MARILYN SINGER

A WASP IS NOT A BEE

Illustrations by
PATRICK O'BRIEN

A TRUMPET CLUB SPECIAL EDITION

INTRODUCTION

Most people know the difference between a cat and a dog. But the differences between certain other animals are not so obvious, which is why people can confuse them. To spot these differences, you have to look and listen carefully, and sometimes use even your other senses.

Observing animals closely can tell you how they vary in size, shape, color, skin, voice, behavior, and other things. It can help you tell not only a wasp from a bee but a spider from an insect, a mammal from a bird.

Some of the animals in this book can be found in your neighborhood. Others are in the zoo, and some you would have to travel to other countries to see. All of them are fascinating. The more you study these and other creatures, the more you can appreciate and enjoy the amazing diversity of the animal kingdom.

A WASP IS

Yellow Jacket

The insect trying to eat your ice-cream cone may look like a bee, but it's probably a yellow-jacket wasp. Some bees and wasps may look similar, but they have many differences. Bees are usually hairy. Wasps are smooth. Most bees can carry pollen on their legs. Wasps can't. The honeybee, which is often confused with the yellow jacket, eats only pollen and nectar. Yellow jackets eat insects and other animals, which they feed their young, and sugary foods like fruit, soda, and your ice-cream cone.

Social bees, such as the honeybee, which live in hives built out of wax, make honey. Social wasps, such as the

NOT A BEE

Honeybee

yellow jacket, which live in nests they make out of paper or other materials, do not. A beehive has many workers and one queen to lay eggs. The queen bee never leaves the hive. A wasp's nest has several queens, and they do leave to hunt food for the young wasps.

To protect their colonies, bees and wasps can both sting. But wasps are usually quicker to do so than bees. One reason for this may be that a honeybee dies after it stings you. But a yellow jacket does not. It can continue to sting you in several places. That's good for the wasp, but not for you.

A SPIDER IS

NOT AN INSECT

When people say, "Ooh, I hate insects," they often mean spiders. But spiders are not insects. They belong to a group called *arachnids*. Insects have six legs, and their bodies have three major sections. Arachnids, which, along with spiders, include mites, ticks, and scorpions, have eight legs, and their bodies have two sections. Most insects have wings and antennae. Spiders, like other arachnids, do not. But they do have a pair of *pedipalps,* which look like short legs, near their jaws. Spiders use these palps to help handle food and in reproduction.

Different insects eat different foods. Some, such as moths and butterflies, have sucking mouths and feed largely on nectar and sap. Others, such as dragonflies, beetles, grasshoppers, and roaches, have chewing mouths to eat a variety of foods, from plants to animals. All spiders are meat eaters, but they can't chew. They paralyze and kill their prey by injecting poison through their fangs and then sucking out the prey's insides.

Only a few spiders have poison that is dangerous to people, and they will not bite unless they are bothered. In fact, spiders are actually very helpful animals. They kill and eat many harmful bugs that, unlike spiders, can really make people's lives miserable.

Jumping Spider

Mottled-Green Mantid

A BAT IS

Pipistrelle

Many people never get to see a bat up close. They see bats only at a distance and confuse them with birds. A close look can tell you why a bat is not a bird but a mammal—the only mammal that flies. Most mammals have at least some hair or fur. The bat's whole body is furry—except for its wings, which are really long, webbed hands and arms. Birds, however, are covered with feathers, including their wings, which are not armlike at all. A bat's mouth is also very different from a bird's. Bats, like many other mammals, have teeth. Birds never do. They have beaks.

All birds lay eggs. These hatch into chicks, which are fed a variety of foods that their parents usually gather for them. Bats do not lay

NOT A BIRD

Eurasian Kestrel

eggs. They give birth to live young, and, like all mammals, they feed their babies milk that mother bats produce in their bodies.

Some bats eat insects, some fruit, others fish, and the vampire bat licks up blood from animals it bites. But no matter what their food, bats do their dining at night. They are all *nocturnal.* Only some birds, such as owls and nighthawks, are awake after dark. Most birds are active during the day. If you see something bird size flutter by you after sundown, it's probably not a bird. More than likely, it's a bat hunting for a mosquito that is looking to make a meal out of you.

A WHALE IS

Sperm Whale

Fish live underwater. If you take a fish out of water for very long, it will die. Whales also live underwater. But if you keep a whale underwater for too long, it will die. That's because a whale is not a fish—it's a mammal. A fish breathes by taking in water and passing it through its gills to extract oxygen. A whale doesn't have gills. Like all mammals, it has lungs. So even though a whale lives in water, it must surface to inhale air through its blowhole, which is really a big nostril on top of its head. A whale's spout is the air it exhales through its blowhole. Some whales have one blowhole; others have two.

Like other mammals, whales have highly developed brains. Unlike other mammals, they do not have body hair, they have smooth skin. A fish has a less complex brain, and it is covered with scales. Another difference between a whale and a fish is that a whale is *warm blooded*. Like all mammals, its body

NOT A FISH

Grunt

temperature stays more or less the same no matter how hot or cold its surroundings are. A fish is *cold blooded.* Its temperature changes with the water temperature.

Whales and fish have streamlined bodies to move easily and quickly through the water. Whales have armlike flippers to help steer and balance them. On their tails they have horizontal, boneless flukes that move up and down. Attached to strong muscles, the flukes propel and steer a whale through the water. Fish do not have flippers or flukes. They have fins, which are usually bony and vertical and move from side to side. A fish gets most of its power for swimming from its whole body. A whale gets its power from its tail. Fish sometimes jump, showing a flash of their tails. But if you see a big, powerful tail thrusting up out of the water, chances are you've just seen a whale.

AN EEL IS

Moray Eel

Ask some people to name a slimy animal, and they might say a snake. But they'd be wrong. A snake is a reptile. A reptile's skin is dry and scaly—or wet and scaly, if it's been swimming—but never slimy. An eel, however, is not a reptile. It's a fish. And all fish are slimy. Like other fish, the eel has scales, but they are so tiny you can't see them. Unlike a snake, which sheds its skin, an eel never sheds.

Some snakes spend a lot of time in the water. Water snakes are good swimmers. But like all reptiles, they have lungs and must come up for air. They also must come out on land to lay their dry, leathery eggs. Eels, like all fish, have gills. They spend their lives in the water and lay their soft, sticky eggs there.

Snakes do not travel far to lay their eggs. The babies, when they hatch, look like adult snakes, only smaller. But some eels, such as freshwater eels, travel great distances from their home lakes and rivers to spawn in the ocean. Newborn eels look nothing like snakes or even grown-up eels. They are transparent and leaflike. They will go through many changes before they become adults. But in their newborn state, they will make the long return trip to the lakes and rivers their parents came from—a truly amazing journey.

NOT A SNAKE

Amazon Tree Boa

A SALAMANDER IS

Red Salamander

The silent, long-tailed lizard-shaped creature caught in your flashlight beam on a nighttime walk through the damp woods is not a lizard. It's a salamander. Lizards are reptiles that are usually found in warm parts of the world, such as deserts or rain forests. Their skin is tough, dry, and scaly. They have claws, and their front feet usually have five toes. They also generally have outer ears. Most lizards are active during the day, and some spend a lot of time sunbathing.

But salamanders are amphibians—cold-blooded animals without scales that are born in the water or moist places. Like other amphibians, salamanders have smooth or warty, delicate and moist skin, which must be protected from the sun. So salamanders are generally nocturnal. Also, unlike lizards, they have four toes on their front feet and no claws at all, and they never have outer ears.

Baby salamanders have gills, and most of them look more like fish than land animals. But as the salamanders grow they change, developing legs and usually losing their gills. Some salamanders live in water, some on land. Others live on both land and water. Although many lizards swim well and some live in water, you're more likely to see a lizard on land—on a tree trunk, in the sand, or perhaps sharing a comfortable, sun-warmed rock with you.

Collared Lizard

A MOTH IS

Spanish Moon Moth

If you see an insect fluttering around an outdoor light on a warm summer night, you're probably watching a moth. Although some moths are day fliers, most fly at night. Most butterflies, however, are active during the day. They need the sunlight to keep their bodies warm. Nocturnal moths have fatter, hairier bodies than butterflies because they can't rely on sunlight for warmth.

Butterflies are often more brightly colored than nocturnal moths, but not always. It's often easier to see the colors and patterns on a butterfly when it flies because a perching butterfly usually keeps its wings folded upright. Moths, on the other hand, generally rest with their wings flat.

Another difference between moths and butterflies is their antennae—the feelers on their heads. Butterflies tend to have little knobs on the ends of their antennae. Moths do not. Their antennae are usually either plain or feathery.

Both moths and butterflies start off as caterpillars. When a caterpillar is full grown, it changes into a *pupa*—the final state before it becomes a butterfly or a moth. Both butterfly and moth caterpillars can spin silk to attach the leaflike pupa to a branch or other support. But only moth caterpillars can spin a *cocoon*—the soft but strong silken case that covers some pupas. Some cocoons are valuable. Silk fabric is made from a silk moth's cocoon. Making silk from a cocoon sounds like magic. But the transformation of a wingless, crawling caterpillar into a graceful, flying butterfly or moth is even more magical.

Monarch Butterfly

A CATERPILLAR

IS NOT A WORM

The worm in your apple is not really a worm at all. It's a caterpillar. People often confuse worms and caterpillars because they both have long, soft bodies with no backbone. If you look at an earthworm, the type of worm you're most likely to see, you'll notice that it's hard to tell which end is the head and which is the tail. You'll also see that the earthworm has no legs. But the caterpillars in your garden usually have distinct heads, and they all have legs.

Garden caterpillars are active during the day. Usually earthworms only come out of their burrows at night because light hurts their sensitive skin. The most important difference between caterpillars and worms is one that is hard to detect: caterpillars change into moths or butterflies; worms always stay worms.

Caterpillars have strong biting jaws to chew plants and other food. They eat a lot and grow fast, shedding their skins several times before they turn into butterflies or moths. Some of them are pests, chomping away at your tomato plants. Others are harmless or useful, feeding on weeds.

Earthworms are always helpful. They live in the soil, which they swallow to extract nourishment. They are good for the soil, loosening and fertilizing it. Earthworms can help make a garden healthy. Caterpillars can destroy a garden. But when they become butterflies and moths, they can also make it beautiful.

Monarch Caterpillar

Earthworm

A GOOSE IS

Canada Goose

Your ears can tell you the difference between a goose and a duck. A goose honks. A duck quacks—or, if it's a whistling duck, it whistles. Your eyes can show you some of the other ways to tell geese and ducks apart. Geese are usually larger than ducks, and they have longer necks and wings. Ducks have flatter bills than geese and their colors are often more striking. Male and female geese look similar. Male and female ducks often look different. The males have the brighter, more colorful feathers. Geese molt—lose their old feathers and grow new ones—once a year. Most ducks molt twice a year.

Geese usually mate for life. Mother geese generally lay five or six eggs at a time, and both parents raise the babies, which

Wood Duck

are called goslings. Most ducks pair up for just a season. Mother ducks lay many more eggs than geese, and they alone care for the ducklings.

Geese mostly graze on land. They are vegetarians, and their high, strong bills are made for cropping grass and other plants. Ducks, however, usually feed in the water. Some ducks are plant eaters. Others eat fish and other seafood. If you go to a lake, you might see a fish-eating duck such as a merganser diving for its food. But a goose, such as the Canada goose, will always dine with you on the shore.

AN ALLIGATOR IS

American Alligator

A person's grin can tell you that he or she is friendly. An alligator's grin can tell you that it's an alligator. Both crocodiles and alligators are large reptiles with big teeth that stick out over their jaws when their mouths are closed. This makes both alligators and crocodiles look as though they're grinning. But only the teeth in an alligator's upper jaw show. Some of a crocodile's bottom teeth stick out as well as its top teeth. Crocodiles' snouts are thin and pointed, while alligators' snouts are broader and more rounded.

Alligators are large and long, and they have loud voices, especially the males. They sound and look ferocious,

NOT A CROCODILE

and they can be. But they don't usually bother people. A crocodile is smaller than an alligator, and its voice is not as powerful. But crocodiles are faster on land and more aggressive. They are more likely to attack you.

Crocodiles and alligators are both fierce hunters, but they are very good and gentle parents. Alligators, which live only in parts of China and the United States, build nests out of plant matter and soil for their hard-shelled eggs. Crocodiles, which can be found in many more places, although rarely in the United States, dig holes for their eggs in sand or dry soil. A crocodile or an alligator is very protective of its eggs and babies. If you ever see one grinning near its nest, watch out. Neither a crocodile nor an alligator's grin is ever really friendly. It's just the way it looks.

Indo-Pacific Crocodile

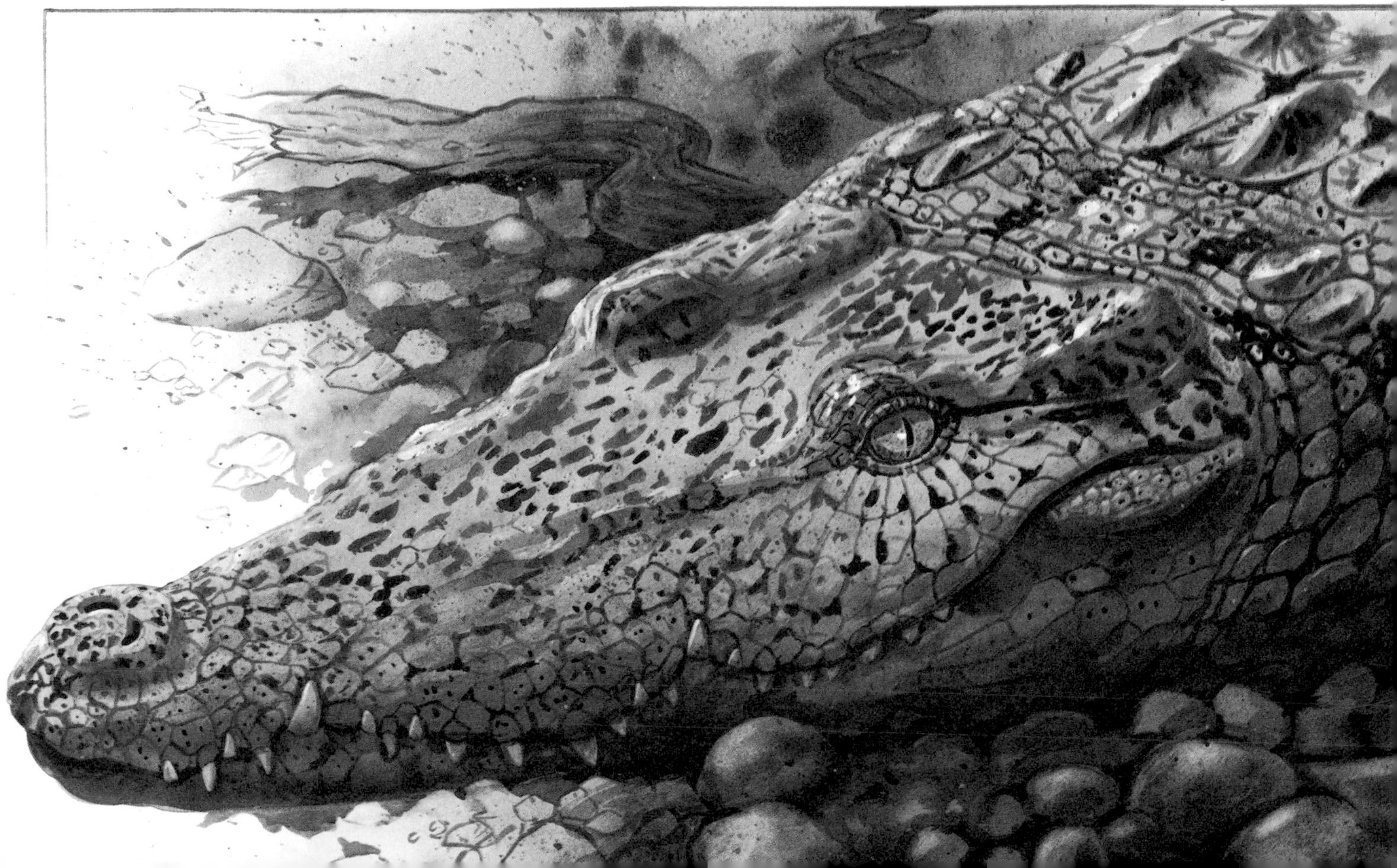

A KOALA IS

Queensland Koala

A koala may look like your favorite teddy bear, but it is not a bear at all. A koala is a marsupial. Like kangaroos, wombats, and opossums, it carries its young in a pouch. Baby koalas are born in the summer and live in their mother's pouch for six to eight months, then ride on her back for a few more months. Bears have no pouch. Their cubs are born during the cold weather in a den where the mother goes for her winter sleep. Most bears, male and female, winter in dens. Koalas never do.

Bears and koalas are also very different in size. Bears are large and powerful. They range from three to nine feet tall and weigh sixty pounds to seventeen hundred pounds or so. The biggest koala is only about two and a half feet tall and weighs under thirty pounds. Both bears and koalas can climb. But

NOT A BEAR

Grizzly Bear

bears spend most of their time on the ground, walking on all four of their feet, and sometimes standing upright on two. Koalas do not walk flat on their feet. In fact, they rarely walk at all. They spend most of their time climbing in the treetops where they sleep and eat.

Koalas eat only one kind of food—the leaves of eucalyptus trees. They even get their water from these leaves. Many eucalyptus trees are found in Australia and nearby islands, which is where koalas live. Bears, however, live all over the world and eat all kinds of food, from fruit and honey to meat. You'd never have to worry about a koala stealing your breakfast. But if you go camping where there are bears, better lock up your grub good and tight.

A HERON IS

A heron is a bird with a long neck, a long bill, and long legs that is often found wading in water. A stork is a bird with a long neck, a long bill, and long legs that is often found wading in water. How can you tell them apart?

Storks are usually bulkier than herons. Their necks are generally thicker and so are their bills, which can be straight or curved. Many storks hunt by putting their big bills in the water and feeling around for their food. The slimmer herons have straight and very pointed bills. Many herons hunt by standing still and watching the water for their prey, then spearing it quickly with their sharp bills.

Herons also often have long, showy feathers on their heads, throats, and backs, especially during the mating season.

Great Blue Heron

NOT A STORK

White Stork

Storks do not have plumes. Many storks even have bare heads.

Storks and herons also look different in flight. All storks fly with their necks stretched straight out. But all herons tuck their heads between their shoulders and curl their necks in an S shape when they fly.

You can also tell herons and storks apart by the sounds they make. Herons make loud, croaking calls often in flight. But many storks are voiceless. Some make just a few calls when they're around their nests. All storks communicate by clapping the two parts of their bills together.

Herons and storks nest in trees. But some storks, such as the white stork, found in Europe and Africa, will also nest on chimneys and rooftops. If you see two big white birds clickety-clacking away at each other on a chimney, you're not imagining things. You've just spotted a pair of storks.

A TOAD IS

NOT A FROG

A toad's skin may be warty, but it can't give you warts. Neither can a frog. Frogs and toads are often hard to tell apart, even for scientists. But true toads, such as the American toad, usually have dry, bumpy skin, while true frogs, such as the bullfrog, generally have wetter, smoother skin. Frogs also have longer legs for leaping and are more streamlined, with narrower waists. Toads, which don't jump as well, have shorter legs for hopping. They are also plumper and broader. Another difference is that frogs have teeth in their upper jaws to grip their food. Toads have no teeth at all.

Both frogs and toads are amphibians. They breed in the water or in moist areas. Their babies, which look like fish, are called tadpoles. Tadpoles eat a lot, grow legs, lose their tails, and turn into little frogs or toads. Most adult frogs spend their time in and near water. Adult toads generally live on land, but they do like a good bath.

True frogs are tasty food to many animals, including some people. True toads are not. That is because toads can produce a bitter-tasting fluid that burns the mouth of an animal that tries to bite it. For protection, frogs most often rely on squawking, leaping, swimming swiftly away, and hiding. A frog is hard to see in the water because it's often the same colors as the green-and-gold water weeds. A toad is hard to spot in the woods because it blends in well with the soil, rocks, and leaves.

Bullfrog

American Toad

Chimpanzee

At the zoo you might see a monkey hanging by its tail. But you'll never see a chimpanzee do that. That's because it doesn't have one. All monkeys have tails. But chimps are not monkeys. They are apes—and no ape ever has a tail. Orangutans, gorillas, and gibbons are also apes. Apes are generally bigger than monkeys. Apes' arms are longer than their legs, and they walk more upright. When they do walk on all fours, most apes, including chimps, support themselves on their knuckles instead of their palms.

Many monkeys live high in the trees, where they eat, play, and sleep. Chimps spend much of their time on the ground, except at night, when they build nests in trees out of leaves

NOT A MONKEY

Squirrel Monkey

and branches. A chimpanzee never uses the same nest twice. It builds a new one every evening.

Monkeys are smart, but chimps are even smarter. They have the most highly developed brains of all apes, perhaps of all mammals other than humans. In fact, of all animals they are the most like people. Chimps make and use simple tools—for example, they will chew leaves and roll them into a ball to use as a sponge to drink from. People have taught sign language to chimps and their cousins, gorillas. These apes learn words easily and can make up sentences. You could have a conversation with a chimp. But you could never have one with a monkey.

To Max, Natasha, and Isaac

—M. S.

To Allison

—P. O. B.

Thanks to Steve Aronson, Shelley Meisler, Brenda Bowen, Simone Kaplan, and the rest of the good folk at Holt. Special thanks to Roland Smith, research biologist and fact-checker supreme.

—M. S.

ISBN 0-590-13904-5

 Published by Scholastic Inc., 555 Broadway, New York, NY 10012, by arrangement with Henry Holt & Company, Inc.

12 11 10 9 8 7 6 5 4 3 2 7 8 9/9 0 1/0

Printed in the U.S.A. 09

The artist used watercolor and gouache on Strathmore bristol board to create the illustrations for this book.